Talking without words

(I can. Can you?)

Written and Illustrated by Marie Hall Ets

THE VIKING PRESS   NEW YORK

To the memory of
May Massee

J
E

Pic Bk
670–69218–2
4 5 6 7 8 79 78 77 76 75

Talking without words

ALSO BY MARIE HALL ETS

The Story of a Baby
In the Forest
Little Old Automobile
Mr. T. W. Anthony Woo
Another Day
Play with Me
Gilberto and the Wind
Automobiles for Mice
Just Me
Elephant
Jay Bird

BY MARIE HALL ETS AND AURORA LABASTIDA

Nine Days to Christmas

"Come here!" I say to my dog. But I don't say it with words.
I just click my tongue and pat my knee and he comes.

"That's *mine*!" says Little Brother when Sister hides his ball from him. But he doesn't say it with words. He just tries to *get* it.

"I want some of whatever it is *you* have," says Old Elephant, but not in words. He just reaches out his trunk and takes some.

"Give me some of your peanuts," says Bear. But he doesn't say it in words. He just opens his mouth and holds up his paw.

"*I* want the rope!" "No, *I* want it!" say Big Brother and Sister,
but without using words. They both hold on to it and both pull.

Sometimes when Mother wants me home in a hurry she doesn't say a word. She just grabs me by the hand and I have to go.

"I love you!" I say to my mother. But I don't say it in words.
I just run and throw my arms around her and hug her.

"Shame on you!" says Sister when I come home crying. But she doesn't shame me with words. She shames me with her fingers.

When Sister won't let me take her scooter I stick out my tongue
to say, "I don't like you!" Then she sticks hers out at me.

"I want to see *them* without their seeing *me*," says Sister, but not in words. She just hides behind the house and peeks.

"Mmmm, that looks good!" say Sister and I as we look at the
birthday cake. But we don't say it in words. We say it like this.

"This soup is too hot!" I say to myself, but without using words.
I just pick up the bowl and blow till the soup is cool.

"Ugh! This apple is sour!" I say to myself after taking a bite.
But I don't say it in words. I just say so by spitting it out.

"I love the smell of flowers!" says Little Brother. But he doesn't say it in words. He just runs and smells whenever he sees some.

When I have a bagful of goodies I don't have to use words.
I just hold it out and Little Brother and Sister both take some.

"Pew! How that stinks!" I say to my dog when he brings home
a dead rat. But I don't say it in words. I just hold my nose.

"I won't take it!" says Little Brother when Mother brings his
medicine. But he doesn't use words. He just covers his mouth.

"Come here. I have something nice for you," says Mother to Little Brother, but not in words. She just motions to him with her finger.

"I hear a bird singing!" says my friend who lives down the street. But he doesn't say it in words. He just stands and listens.

When Big Brother and I want a fight we don't say so with words.
We can say so better with our fists—like this.

"Good-by," Little Brother says to Mother before running to play.
But he doesn't say it in words. He just comes and kisses her.

"Throw it to *me too*!" says Little Brother when Big Brother and
Sister are playing ball. But he just says it with his hands.

When I'm too hot I take off my coat. When Sister's too cold she hugs herself and shivers. We don't need to use words to say so.

"Look!" I say when my bubble goes way up to the top of the tree. But I don't *say* the word, I just point. And Little Sister looks.

"Don't wake the baby," says Mother, but without using words.
She just puts a finger on her lips and Little Brother understands.

"Good-by!" I wave as you go away. You are too far for words, so I only hope you'll turn around and wave good-by to me.

"I don't want to hear!" says Little Brother when Mother starts scolding. But he doesn't say it in words. He just covers his ears.

"Where's your jacket?" Mother asks when I come home. But I don't know. So I just shrug my shoulders and hold out my hands.